Soul Slasher

I Always Love My Mama

Written by

Curtis Harrison

Table of Contents

Chapter 1

A dimly lit apartment window flickered with a dull glow from a streetlight outside. It was night in Detroit, Michigan, sometime in the 1970s.

Young Darius Whitaker, just seven years old, wide-eyed and trembling, peeks from behind a cracked bedroom door. His mother, Evelyn, in her mid-30s, bruised and exhausted, is pressed against the wall. Her husband, Hank, in his 40s, drunk and cruel, stands over her, his belt clenched in one fist, a bottle of Jack in the other.

"You think you can talk back to me?" Hank says.

Hank throws the bottle, shattering glass across the kitchen floor. Evelyn flinches but says nothing. Hank grabs her by the hair and yanks her toward him.

Darius clutches a tiny clown figurine in his small hands, trembling. His fingers dig into the painted face.

"Take those damn pants off," Hank says.

Evelyn locks eyes with her son through the cracked door. A silent plea.

"Darius, baby, go to bed—" Evelyn says.

CRACK! The belt lashes against her back, her scream muffled by Hank's heavy hand. Darius covers his ears. Tears streak his face. His mother's muffled cries rip through the silence.

Darius backs away. His foot catches a toy car— CRUNCH.

Hank hears it. His head snaps up, bloodshot eyes locking onto the cracked door.

"Boy, you best not be watchin'," Hank says.

Darius whimpers and stumbles back—but Hank is already stomping toward him. The door swings open. Hank looms over Darius, the belt dripping from his fist.

"You wanna be next?" Hank says.

Darius freezes, and everything goes black in an instant.

Months later, Eight-year-old Darius is sitting silently in the backseat of the car, clutching his clown figurine, staring out the window. Evelyn drives, her lip busted, one eye swollen shut.

"We're gonna be okay, baby," Evelyn says.

She grips the wheel tightly, checking the rearview mirror. No sign of Hank.

"We're gonna start fresh—" Evelyn says.

Blinding lights. A truck slams into the car. Metal crunches. Glass shatters. Blackness. Muffled screams. Sirens. Darius sits up in bed, his neck in a brace, bruises along his arms.

A doctor in his 50s, sympathetic, sits beside Evelyn.

"The trauma from the crash… he's not speaking," the doctor says.

Evelyn looks at Darius, heartbreak in her eyes.

"Darius, baby… say somethin'," Evelyn says.

Darius stares blankly at his clown figurine. Silent.

The doctor places a hand on Evelyn's shoulder.

"Sometimes, the mind protects itself," the doctor says.

Darius just stares.

Everything fades to black. Eleven years later, 18-year-old Darius Whitaker leans against a flickering streetlight, wearing bell-bottom jeans, an Afro pick in his hair, and a 70s-style leather jacket. It was a cold night in Detroit in 1988.

His eyes are distant, stuck in another time. Music blares from a club down the block. Across the street, a pregnant woman in her 20s stumbles backward; a man in his 30s, aggressive, grabs her by the wrist.

"Don't you walk away from me!" the man says.

She tries to pull free. He slaps her—hard. Darius stiffens. Something snaps inside him. He crosses the street, hands in his pockets.

"Please… stop—" the pregnant woman says.

The man raises his fist again—Darius moves fast. Grabs a bottle from the gutter and smashes it against a mailbox. The sharp glass flashes as he lunges forward and stabs him. The man gasps, eyes wide. Blood spurts from his side. Darius doesn't stop. *Stab. Stab. Stab.* The woman starts screaming.

Darius keeps going. He stabbed him fifteen times, and the blood coats his hands and his face. The glass slips from his fingers. Sirens wail in the distance as the woman backs away, horrified. Darius just stands there, breathing heavily, looking at the man crumpled in the street.

The 70s music still plays from the club.

"Put your hands where I can see 'em!" a police officer shouts.

Red and blue lights flood the scene. Darius doesn't run. He just closes his eyes… and smiles.

Everything smashes to black and weeks later, in the courtroom, the judge in his 50s sternly glares down at Darius, who sits in handcuffs, expression blank.

"Darius Whitaker, you are found guilty of murder in the second degree," the judge says.

Evelyn, now older, exhausted, and broken, sits in the gallery, tears streaming down her face.

"You are hereby sentenced to life in prison," the judge declares.

Darius doesn't react. Two guards cuff him and escort him away. As he passes Evelyn, he briefly looks at her.

"I love you, baby," Evelyn whispers.

Darius lowers his head. The guards lead him into the darkness.

Chapter 2

Everything fades to black, and thirty-two years later, it's 2025, and Darius Whitaker is now in his 50s, sitting on his prison cell's bunk, staring at the yellowed newspaper in his lap. His fingers trace the bold headline:

"DETROIT WOMAN FOUND DEAD. BOYFRIEND SUSPECTED."

A grainy photo of his mother, Evelyn Whitaker.

His Afro is graying. His hands are rough. A tiny radio on the shelf plays a Delfonics song, warbling from age. He grips the paper so tightly that it crumples.

"That your people?" the inmate asks.

The inmate in his 40s, skinny, tattooed hands, sits on the bottom bunk, watching. Darius doesn't answer.

"Man, I'm sorry—" the inmate says.

THWACK! Darius suddenly punches the wall, HARD. The impact splits his knuckles. Blood seeps down his fingers. The radio crackles as The Delfonics fade into silence. Darius clenches his fists, struggling to breathe. He grabs his throat as if trying to push the pain back down.

Then, a guttural scream rips out of him. RAW. PAINED. ANIMALISTIC. The inmate flinches, backing away.

"Yo, man, calm down—" the inmate mumbles.

Darius lunges at him and grabs him by the collar. His breath is hot, furious.

"Who?" Darius asks in a raspy, whispering voice.

The inmate shakes his head, terrified.

"Man, I—I don't know—" the inmate says.

Darius shoves him back onto the bunk. Staggers to the sink, splashing cold water on his face. He looks in the tiny, cracked mirror. For a moment, his younger self stares back at him. The kid who watched Hank beat his mother. The kid who stayed silent. His breath shudders. His fists tighten. He won't be silent this time.

Chapter 3

Later, Darius walks through the prison yard in the morning with his head down. He passes a group of inmates playing dominoes, laughing. They stop talking when they see him.

"Yo, Whitaker lookin' mad different today," the inmate says.

"That man got death in his eyes," another inmate adds.

Darius keeps walking. His mind is somewhere else. Up ahead—the guards' entrance. A locked steel door. Two guards stand in front of it. Darius stares, studying and memorizing. His fingers tap against his thigh, following a rhythm. The same rhythm his mother used to hum when she cleaned the house. A new plan forms in his mind.

Darius sits on the bunk of his prison cell in the night, focused, hands wrapped in cloth like a fighter preparing for battle. A shank—fashioned from a sharpened toothbrush—rests beside him. He picks up a stolen keycard.

From his window, he watches the guards rotate shifts. He's memorized the schedule. His breathing slows. He rubs his hands together. Then—he moves.

Inside the prison hallway at night, A guard in his 50s, tired and overweight, walks down the hallway, humming an old blues song. Darius emerges from the shadows behind him before the guard can react—SLICE.

The shank rips across his throat. The guard's eyes go wide. He drops, clutching his neck, gurgling. Darius drags the body into the dark.

A moment later, inside the locker room, Darius zips up the guard's uniform. He checks himself in the mirror—he looks good. The Afro doesn't fit the image, though. He grabs a hat from the dead guard's locker. Puts it on. Now, he looks official. He keeps the keycard in his pocket and moves further.

Soon after, at the prison checkpoint, a young rookie guard in his 22, nervous, sits behind a monitor. Darius walks up, keeping his head down.

"You on night shift?" the rookie guard asks.

Darius nods and hands him the keycard. The guard swipes it. The screen beeps.

"You uh… new?" the guard asks.

Darius just grunts and keeps walking. The guard watches him go. Something feels off.

Darius steps outside in the prison parking lot, breathing in fresh air for the first time in years. A prison van sits nearby. Darius casually walks toward it. Behind him—the prison alarm blares. "ESCAPE ATTEMPT IN PROGRESS."

Darius doesn't hesitate. He jumps into the van, and the tires screech as they peel away. He peels out, vanishing into the night.

Darius drives in the streets of Detroit with one hand, his other gripping the wheel tight. The city hasn't changed. Still dirty. Still loud. The radio crackles. An old James Brown song plays. Darius smirks. He's home. But he ain't here for nostalgia. He's here for revenge.

Darius stares up at an old, run-down apartment complex. He clutches a piece of paper—his mother's last known address. His jaw tightens. He heads inside.

A knock at the door. A man in his 40s, greasy, cocky, opens the apartment door. This is Rodney Blake. The man who killed Evelyn Whitaker. Rodney blinks. Sees a man in a guard uniform, hat pulled low.

"Yo, what's this about?" Rodney asks.

Darius slowly lifts his head. Rodney's eyes widen. Darius steps inside. Shuts the door and locks it. Rodney laughs nervously.

"Look, man—" Rodney says.

WHAM. Darius punches him. HARD. Rodney stumbles back, coughing.

"Hold up—" Rodney says.

Darius grabs him by the throat and slams him against the wall. His eyes are dark and cold.

"Did she beg?" Darius asks in a low, rasping voice.

Rodney chokes.

"Did she scream?" Darius asks.

Rodney claws at Darius' hands.

"Wait—wait—" Rodney says.

Darius reaches into his jacket. Pulls out the shank. Rodney's eyes go wide.

"Let's find out," Darius says.

A bloody handprint smears the wall. Rodney's body lies slumped on the floor, lifeless. Darius sits on the couch, breathing heavily. A cigarette burns in the ashtray. He looks at his bloody hands. The radio plays soft soul music. Then, Darius leans back and closes his eyes. For the first time in decades—he feels free.

15

Chapter 4

A small, dingy motel room. The neon glow from outside flickers through the blinds, casting ghostly red and blue lines across the walls. Darius stands in front of the bathroom mirror, washing his bloodstained hands. His breathing is steady now. The storm in his head has quieted, but his eyes burn with something new. He reaches into his jacket pocket and pulls out a crumpled matchbook.

The address scrawled inside: "Rockwell Bar, 49th & Main. Friday Nights." He knows the name, Freddie "Blaze" Henderson, the man who murdered his mother. Darius' jaw clenches. A song begins to play on the motel radio, *"I Always Love My Momma"* by The Intruders. Darius slowly turns the volume up. He closes his eyes and listens to the song. Tomorrow, he finds Freddie. Tomorrow, he ends this.

The Rockwell Bar is a hole-in-the-wall dive with flickering neon signs and peeling paint. Inside, the music is loud and bass-heavy. Drunken laughter spills out onto the street. Darius sits in a car across the street, watching. He lights a cigarette. From the entrance, a man stumbles out—mid-40s, cocky grin, expensive rings. This is Freddie "Blaze" Henderson. Darius' stomach twists.

He grips the steering wheel so hard his knuckles turn white. He watches and waits. Finally, Freddie heads toward the alley behind the bar. Darius flicks the cigarette away. It's time.

Behind Rockwell Bar, the alley was dark, and there Freddie unzips his fly, pissing against the brick wall. He's drunk, mumbling to himself.

Darius steps out of the shadows. Freddie notices too late.

"The fuck you lookin' at, old man?" Freddie shouts.

Darius doesn't answer. Just keeps walking toward him, slow and deliberate. Freddie snorts.

"I said, the fu—" Freddie says.

THWACK. Darius smashes a lead pipe across Freddie's jaw. Freddie collapses, coughing blood.

"MOTHERFUCKER!" Freddie shouts.

Darius kneels beside him.

"Did she beg?" Darius asks in a low and raspy voice.

Freddie's eyes widen.

"Did she scream?" Darius asks again.

Freddie groans, dazed.

"What—who—?" Freddie says.

CRACK. Darius slams his head against the pavement. Freddie wheezes.

"You killed Evelyn Whitaker," Darius says.

Freddie's expression shifts, a mix of realization and panic crossing his face. "Look, man—" Freddie mumbles.

Darius grabs his hair, dragging him deeper into the alley. Freddie struggles.

"WAIT! WAIT! I didn't mean to!" Freddie screams.

Darius slams his fist into his gut.

"I don't care what you meant," Darius says.

He pulls out a rusty hunting knife. Freddie freezes.

"Oh shit," Freddie says.

Darius smiles. Soon after, Freddie is tied to a chair inside an abandoned warehouse, bloodied and shaking. Darius paces in front of him, methodical and controlled.

"She was my mother," Darius says.

Freddie whimpers. Darius kneels beside him.

"And you took her from me," Darius added.

Freddie sobs. Darius reaches into his pocket. Pulls out a small jar of white face paint. Freddie stares in confusion.

"Wha—what the fuck?" Freddie shouts.

Darius dips his fingers into the paint. Begins smearing it across Freddie's face. Slowly. Carefully. Freddie shakes, terrified.

"Please, man—" Freddie begs.

Darius paints two big red circles on his cheeks.

"Smile for me," Darius whimpers.

He cuts both sides of Freddie's mouth. Freddie screams, blood pouring down his chin. Darius paints over the wounds, finishing the clown face.

"There. That's better," Darius says.

Freddie sobs. Shaking. Darius steps back. Admiring his work.

He turns on the radio. "I Always Love My Momma" plays softly. Darius grins.

"Let's dance," Darius says.

Freddie screams as the knife comes down.

Darius stands in front of a cracked mirror. His face is covered in blood. In his hands—Freddie's face, peeled clean off. He lifts it slowly. Presses it against his own skin. Ties it in place with a thin wire. The bloody clown's face stares back at him. Darius tilts his head. A slow and eerie smile spreads across his lips. For the first time in decades—he feels complete.

Darius walks in the streets of Detroit at night, his new face dripping blood onto the pavement. The city lights flicker. The world feels different now. His heartbeat is calm. His purpose is clear. He pulls a crumpled newspaper from his pocket. A headline catches his eye:

"MAN CHARGED IN CHILD ABUSE CASE RELEASED EARLY."

Darius smiles beneath the mask. His fingertips graze the newspaper's ink. A new mission forms in his mind.

"I see you," Darius says softly to himself.

A dimly lit, filthy motel room. The television flickers with static. The air reeks of cheap cigarettes and whiskey. Darius sits on the bed, scrolling through his stolen laptop. On the screen: a list of convicted abusers. His fingers move steadily, clicking, scanning, and selecting. Then, he stops. A mugshot fills the screen—GARY "BIG G" MATTHEWS. Convicted of beating his girlfriend and her 6-year-old son. Released last month.

Darius stares at the photo. Memorizes every line of the man's face. Then, he grabs his duffel bag and stands. A seedy and smoke-filled dive bar. The neon sign flickers erratically. Inside, the jukebox plays an old country tune. Darius leans against the wall outside, watching. Waiting. The door swings open. A large, scruffy man stumbles out, laughing drunkenly with a friend. Gary Matthews. He slaps his friend's back, reeking of booze.

"Nother round?" Gary asks.

His friend shakes his head. "Man, I'm tapped out. You good?" the friend says.

"I'm always good, baby," Gary answers.

He laughs, heading toward his truck. Darius follows from a distance.

Later at night, Gary fumbles with his keys at his apartment door. Darius stands in the shadows, watching. Gary finally gets the door open and stumbles inside. Darius waits for a few beats before he finally moves.

Inside the cheap, cluttered apartment. Beer cans on the table. Dirty clothes everywhere. Gary plops onto the couch, sighing. He doesn't notice Darius emerging from the darkness, not until—SLAM.

Darius presses a gloved hand over his mouth, stabbing him in the thigh. Gary screams into the glove, thrashing. Darius leans in, whispering.

"Shh," Darius says.

Gary's eyes widen. Darius removes his hand.

"WHO THE FU—" Gary shouts.

THWACK. Darius slams a hammer into his jaw. Gary spits blood, choking and trembling. Darius walks to the record player. He pulls out a vinyl record. Slowly, he places it on the turntable. A scratchy melody fills the room—*"I Always Love My Momma"* by The Intruders.

Gary wheezes, crawling toward the door. Darius grabs him by the hair.

"You like hurting women?" Darius asks.

Gary whimpers. Darius tightens his grip.

"Like hurting kids?" Darius asks again.

Gary shakes his head violently.

"NO! NO, PLEASE!" Gary begs.

Darius smiles under his bloodied clown mask.

"Liar," Darius added.

And then, the knife sinks into Gary's neck. Blood spurts onto the walls. Gary gurgles and twitches. Darius kneels beside him, watching. The music plays on. Darius hums along. *"I always love my momma..."*

Gary takes his last breath. Darius leaves the record spinning. Then, he walks out into the night.

Later, in a quiet and upper-class neighborhood. Streetlights buzz faintly. Darius sits in a stolen car, watching a house across the street. He checks his notebook. Inside, a name is scribbled: Martin Webb. He was convicted of molesting his 9-year-old niece. Released after serving only two years. Darius cracks his knuckles, he waits.

Chapter 5

Martin Webb's house is modern and clean. Everything is perfectly arranged. He sips whiskey in front of the TV alone at night. His wife and kids are out of town. He sighs and stretches, completely unaware.

He hears a creak sound and pauses. He looks toward the hallway. There is only silence. He shrugs, turns back to the TV. Another creak came from closer. Martin grabs the remote and mutes the TV.

His breath hitches.

"...Hello?" Martin says.

There is only silence.

He grabs a fireplace poker. Slowly, he moves toward the hallway. Darkness ahead, but then a shadow shifts. Martin's heartbeat pounds.

"Who's there?!" Martin shouts.

He hears nothing. He swallows hard and steps forward. Suddenly, a soft chuckle echoes from the darkness. Martin freezes. His hand tightens on the poker.

"I'll call the cops!" he yells.

A voice from the darkness came. "Call them," Darius replies.

Martin's blood runs cold. He lunges forward, swinging the poker. Then, a hand grabs his wrist. Before he can react, Darius pulls him into the darkness.

Soon after, Martin finds himself inside his basement with dim lighting. Martin is strapped to a chair. His mouth was duct-taped.

Darius paces slowly in front of him. Bloodstains smear his clown mask. He's holding a photo of a little girl.

"She trusted you," Darius says.

Martin shakes violently, tears streaming down his face.

"And you took that trust," Darius continues.

Martin muffles screams through the tape.

Darius pulls out a knife slowly. Martin shrieks, struggling against the restraints.

"Tell me something," Darius says and then leans in. "Do you feel fear?" he whispers.

Martin nods frantically. Darius nods too.

"Good," Darius says.

Then, the blade plunges into Martin's stomach. Blood pours down his shirt as his body jerks violently. Darius tilts his head, watching. He grabs a paintbrush and dips it in Martin's own blood. Turning to the wall, he slowly draws a big, bloody smile. Martin wheezes, then goes still. Darius steps back, admiring his artwork. Then, he turned toward the door.

As he walks out, he whispers, "Sweet dreams."

At the police station, the homicide unit is a cramped and cluttered office. The walls are lined with photos of crime scenes.

Detective Malik Turner, a sharp and intense man in his forties with a no-nonsense demeanor, sips his cold coffee while keeping his eyes locked on the whiteboard. Across from him, Detective Lisa Ramos, a methodical and sharp-witted woman in her thirties, flips through a case file with focused precision.

The whiteboard shows three victims: Gary Matthews, a domestic abuser, found with a vinyl record playing.

Martin Webb, a child molester, was found with a bloody clown smile on the wall. A third man—same pattern. Ramos sets the file down.

"You see what I see?" she asks.

Turner nods, rubbing his temple. "They all deserved it," he says.

Ramos raises a brow. "We don't get to decide that," she says.

Turner leans back and sighs. "Someone out there thinks they do," he adds.

She flips a page and taps a crime scene photo. "Three bodies. Same execution style. Same... signature."

She gestures to a blurry surveillance screenshot. It shows a figure walking down a dark street, wearing a bloodied clown mask, an Afro, and a long coat.

Turner leans forward. "Clown mask. Afro. Like some twisted ass Blaxploitation villain."

Ramos exhales. "Whoever this guy is... he's got a code."

Turner nods slowly. "Yeah. And that makes him dangerous."

Later at the police station in a meeting room, Turner and Ramos sit across from Captain Ray Monroe, who is in his fifties, a weary, old-school cop.

Monroe flips through the case file and sighs. "You're telling me some vigilante is running around carving up dirtbags?"

Turner nods. "And he's getting bolder."

Monroe grunts, tossing the file down. "You think the public's gonna shed tears over dead rapists and wife beaters?"

Ramos crosses her arms. "This isn't about sympathy. This is about control. He's making the rules now."

Monroe studies them. "So, stop him before this turns into a goddamn movement."

After a small pause, Turner picks up the file and says. "We'll find him."

Later, outside a luxury high-rise apartment complex, sleek and imposing. Through the glass windows of the penthouse, we glimpse James Callaway—a wealthy, smug businessman in his fifties, exuding the confidence of someone who believes he's untouchable.

He sips bourbon while watching the news. On screen: a segment covering the recent vigilante murders.

Callaway's jaw tightens. He turns to his bodyguard, Vince—a large, ex-military man standing nearby. "You think this psycho's real?" Callaway asks.

Vince shrugs. "Three dead ain't a myth," he replies.

Callaway swirls his bourbon, smirking. "He's got balls. I'll give him that."

Vince shifts uncomfortably. "The cops say he's only going after abusers," he says.

Callaway laughs. "You worried, Vince?"

Vince doesn't laugh. "You should be," he replies.

Callaway's smirk fades. "That's why I have you," he says.

Vince nods. "I'll keep my eyes on you. No one's getting in," he assures him.

Callaway raises his glass. "Then, let the bastard come," he says.

At night, near Callaway's building, Darius watches through binoculars from the rooftop. He sees Callaway laughing, drinking, and feeling untouchable. Darius pulls out his notebook.

Under Callaway's name, he writes: Tomorrow night."

He closes the notebook. Whispers to himself, "See you soon," Darius says.

Soon after, outside the Callaway's mansion. A gated estate with security cameras and armed guards patrolling. A black Lamborghini is parked in the driveway. From the tree line, Darius watches. His breath fogs in the cold air. He tilts his head, calculating. Slowly, he pulls out a folded map of the estate. A smile creeps beneath the bloodied clown mask. He tucks the map away. Time to go to work.

Inside Callaway's bedroom, James Callaway stands in front of a mirror, adjusting his tie. Behind him, his wife, Clarissa, in her forties, elegant but distant, sits at a vanity, removing her earrings.

Their ten-year-old son, Jason—quiet and fearful of his father—peeks timidly from the hallway. Callaway catches sight of him in the mirror's reflection.

"Go to bed, Jason," Callaway says.

Jason hesitates. "...Dad?" he asks.

Callaway turns, irritated. "What?" he snaps.

Jason swallows hard. "Is that man really coming for you?" he asks.

Callaway chuckles. "Let me tell you something, son." He walks to Jason, kneels down, and forces a firm grip on his shoulder.

"Nobody can touch me," Callaway says.

Jason nods, scared. Callaway pats his cheek, maybe too hard.

"Now, bed," Callaway orders.

Jason scurries away, then Callaway turns back to the mirror.

Then, a faint scratching sound. He freezes and turns toward the open balcony door. A gust of wind blows the curtains. Callaway narrows his eyes.

"Vince?!" Callaway calls out.

There is nothing but silence. He strides to the door, and a shadow moves. Callaway spins around, but it's too late. A gloved hand clamps over his mouth. A knife buries deep into his ribs.

After a while, inside the security room, three armed guards watch the mansion's security monitors.

"Yo, where's Vince?" Guard one asks.

The second guard taps his earpiece. "Vince, check in," he says.

There is only silence.

"That's not good," Guard one mutters.

He switches to another camera feed.

On the screen: A figure in a bloodied clown mask stares directly into the camera. The figure is holding up Vince's severed hand. The guards barely react before the power cuts out. Total darkness, a beat, then a scream from upstairs.

Callaway chokes on his own blood in his room, collapsing to the floor. Darius looms over him.

His clown mask is painted with fresh crimson. Clarissa screams, backing away. Darius tilts his head.

"Shhh," Darius says softly.

Clarissa freezes.

Callaway, still alive, sputters. Darius kneels beside him, lifting his knife.

"You used to tell them to shut up, didn't you?" Darius says.

Callaway shakes violently, trying to speak.

"Their cries. Their pleas," Darius says. Darius grabs Callaway's jaw, forcing it open. "Let's take that away."

Callaway shrieks as Darius plunges the knife into his mouth. A sickening rip. Blood pools on the floor. Darius lifts Callaway's severed tongue, inspecting it.

"No more talking," Darius says.

He drops the tongue onto Callaway's chest. Life fades away from Callaway's eyes.

Darius turns to Clarissa. She trembles, covering her mouth. Jason stands in the doorway, eyes wide with terror.

Darius meets Jason's gaze. "You don't have to be like him."

Jason nods slowly. Darius steps past him, disappearing into the dark hallway.

The sound of a vinyl record starts playing. "I Always Love My Momma" fills the mansion.

The gates of Callaway's mansion swing open. Darius walks down the driveway, drenched in blood. The mansion burns behind him. Flames lick the night sky. He keeps walking, not looking back.

Chapter 6

New York City hums with life under neon lights. TV screens in storefronts, bars, and news stations blast the latest headlines.

Televisions across different locations broadcast the same news report. A female news anchor stares at the camera. "The city is in shock tonight as yet another violent killing has been linked to the now-infamous 'Soul Slasher.'"

TV Screen Montage shows Rapid Clips. Callaway's burned mansion. Cops and reporters are flooding the crime scene. A sketch of the killer's eerie clown mask with a bloodied smile. A vinyl record found at the scene, still playing *I Always Love My Momma*.

The anchor's voice continues over the footage.

"The masked killer, who leaves behind 70s music at every crime scene, has sparked a citywide debate—"

Later, inside a dive bar, a group of blue-collar men drink and argue over the news.

"I'm tellin' ya, he's cleaning up the trash!" one man says.

"Yeah, well, murder's still murder," says another.

"Tell that to the women those bastards beat half to death," the third man says.

The bartender shakes his head. "I dunno, man. You start pickin' and choosin' who deserves to die, where does it end?" he says.

A drunk man in a corner booth grins. "It doesn't end. That's the whole damn point."

They all fall silent. The jukebox plays a slow 70s track. The drunk smiles. "I like this guy," he says.

Inside the NYPD Homicide Unit, Detective Ray Holloway, in his fifties, rugged, haunted by past cases, sits at his cluttered desk. The walls are covered in crime scene photos. The clown mask sketch is pinned up in the center. He stares at it.

"What the hell are you trying to tell me?" Holloway mutters.

Detective Julia Reyes, in her forties, sharp, no-nonsense, enters, tossing a file on his desk. "I think I found something," she says.

Holloway opens the file. Inside, DARIUS WHITAKER was written, along with his prison records and his mugshot.

"Who is this?" Holloway asks.

"Darius Whitaker. Convicted of murder in 1988. Stabbed a guy fifteen times," Reyes says.

Holloway nods, flipping through the papers.

"Here's the kicker," Reyes adds, leaning in. "He escaped six months ago."

Holloway's jaw tightens. "And we're just finding out now?"

"He killed three guards on the way out. Feds kept it under wraps to avoid panic," Reyes says.

Holloway leans back, rubbing his temples. "Jesus."

Reyes points to the file. "Check this out."

Holloway reads the details. His eyes widened. "His mother was murdered..."

"Two weeks before he escaped," Reyes says.

With a beat, Holloway closes the file. "Where does he go next?"

Later, inside a dimly lit motel room with peeling wallpaper. A portable record player spins vinyl. Darius sits on the edge of the bed. His clown mask rests beside him. His eyes flicker with something deep. He pulls out a folded list.

The next name: "HAROLD LANGSTON – CHILD PREDATOR." Darius folds the paper. The music keeps playing. Outside, a police siren wails, and Darius closes his eyes.

Detective Holloway stands on the city streets at night, leaning against his car, smoking a cigarette. Reyes steps beside him.

"What's the plan?" Reyes asks.

"We need to find people who knew him," Holloway says.
He flicks the cigarette. "And we should pray we're not too late."

The next morning, in a nursing home, an elderly woman, Ms. Gardner, in her eighties, with a sharp memory, sips her tea.

Holloway and Reyes sit across from her. She studies the mugshot.

"Darius..." she says softly.

"You knew him?" Holloway asks.

"I taught him in grade school. Quiet boy," Ms. Gardner says. She pauses. "Smart. But there was always... something," she adds.

Reyes leans in. "Like what?"

Ms. Gardner sets down her tea. "Pain."

There's a pause for a moment, and then she adds. "His stepfather was a monster."

Holloway exchanges a look with Reyes.

"That boy suffered more than most," Ms. Gardner continues.

After a long silence, she touches the mugshot gently and adds. "But I never thought he'd become this."

Outside Darius' old neighborhood, the street is run-down and quiet in the daylight. Kids play basketball nearby. Holloway and Reyes knock on a door.

A woman in her mid-fifties answers.

"Yeah?" she says.

"We're looking for information on Darius Whitaker," Holloway says.

She stiffens and adds. "That name's been dead for a long time."

Holloway pulls out the mugshot. "Not anymore."

The woman stares at it in a long silence. "What did he do?" she asks.

Reyes hesitates. "You watch the news?"

The woman closes her eyes. She nods slowly and says. "I knew this day was coming."

Holloway leans forward. "Tell us what you know."

She takes a deep breath. "He wasn't born a killer." After a pause, the woman adds. "But the world made him one."

One moment after another passes, and the story about him keeps growing. A graffiti mural appears in the city, Darius' clown mask was painted like a saint. Social media explodes with debates: Is he a hero or a monster? Protesters march, chanting his name. Others demand justice.

Late-night hosts mock the police for failing to catch him. Underground forums call him the "soul of vengeance." A radio talk show host argues: "What's worse? A murderer… or the people he kills?"

Chapter 7

Darius watches the news at his hideout at night. He sees the graffiti of himself. A strange look crosses his face. He turns to his reflection in the mirror. His bloodied clown mask stares back. He tilts his head.

A whisper escapes his lips. "...They see me now."

The record player clicks, a new song starts, and Darius smiles.

Later at night, inside an abandoned motel room, A flickering neon light buzzes. Darius sits on the edge of the bed, breathing heavily. A bloody knife rests on the nightstand. His clown mask lies beside it.

The record player spins vinyl. A soft, eerie 70s soul music plays. Suddenly, a woman laughs..

"You did good, baby," a woman says.

Darius tenses, and he turns his head. In the dim light, his mother stands by the window.

"You always were my strong boy," Darius' mother says while smiling.

Darius stares, breath shaky. His mother looks just like she did when he was a child. Soft curls with warm brown eyes. Then, she tilts her head.

"Aren't you gonna come hug me?" Darius' mother asks.

Darius' lips tremble. "...Mom?" he whispers.

After a brief pause, a flashback hits him like a wave.

It's 1975. Inside a small, dimly lit apartment, the television flickers in the corner, playing a rerun of "Soul Train."

Little Darius, just eight years old, sits on the floor, coloring in a notebook. The music tries to drown out the yelling coming from the bedroom. Then, the door slams open.

His stepfather, James, a brutish, drunk man in his mid-40s, storms out. Darius' mother stumbles behind him, holding her cheek.

"Don't talk back to me, woman!" James slurs, staggering.

Darius drops his crayon. His mother forces a smile, lips split and bleeding. She kneels beside him, gently stroking his hair.

"It's okay, baby," she whispers.

James scoffs, grabbing a beer from the kitchen counter. "Boy's gonna grow up soft if you keep coddling him," he sneers.

Darius grips his mother's dress tightly. She leans down, whispering again, even softer this time.

"One day, baby… we're gonna get out of here." She kisses his forehead.

James laughs, cold and cruel. "Over my dead body."

Darius jolts back to reality. His mother still stands by the window, watching him.

"I told you, baby… one day, we'd be free," she says gently.

Darius closes his eyes, his body trembling. "I tried, Mama…" he murmurs.

She steps forward. "But you're not done yet," she pauses before adding. "He's still out there."

Darius' eyes snap open. "Who?" he asks.

Her smile fades. "Him."

His breath hitches. The shadows start to swallow her.

"Find him," she says as her image fades completely.

A long silence. Then, the record scratches. The song skips. Darius slowly stands. His hands clenched into fists. His mother's voice echoes in his head.

"Find him," Darius' mother says.

Later that night, Darius sits at a computer at the city library. His fingers tremble as he types on Google search: "James Whitaker New York"

The screen loads. His heart pounds like a war drum. Then, a result pops up: James Whitaker – Resident At Willow Oak Retirement Home. His hand hovers over the mouse. His chest rises and falls. Then, a slow grin spreads across his face.

Soon after, Darius is at the Willow Oak Retirement Home, a quiet building on the outskirts of the city. A soft breeze rustles the trees. Streetlights hum gently overhead. From across the street, Darius watches. A white-haired man sits on the front porch. A nurse helps him sip tea.

Darius' jaw tightens. It's James Whitaker, old, fragile, and weak.

"You thought you'd get to die peacefully," Darius says.

His hand grips the knife in his coat pocket, and after a moment, he steps forward.

Stillness blankets the building. The chirp of insects. The flicker of a dying streetlight. Darius stands in the shadows. Eyes locked on James. The old man rocks gently in his chair. The nurse helps him with the tea. James coughs, his hands trembling. The once-powerful frame is now reduced to skin and bone.

Darius clenches his fists tighter.

"You're supposed to be dead," Darius says in a soft and dark tone.

The nurse pats James on the shoulder. "Let's get you inside, Mr. Whitaker."

James nods slowly, staring into the distance. "Storm's coming," he mutters.

Darius tilts his head. There's already a chill in the air. The storm is here.

Later, inside the old home, A dim hallway stretches ahead. Soft beeps echo from heart monitors. Nurses whisper as they pass, unaware.

Darius moves through the corridor like a ghost. A clipboard hangs on the wall: Room 16B – James Whitaker.

He touches the name with his fingers. His breath slows, controlled, and focused.

He pushed to open the door.

Chapter 8

A dark room named 16-B, filled with the scent of antiseptic and old age. It's night, and James Whitaker lies in bed, his chest rising and falling weakly. His wrinkled hands tremble as he adjusts his oxygen mask. In the corner, a vinyl record player sits untouched, covered in dust.

Darius steps forward, and a floorboard creaks. James stirs, his eyes flutter open. For a moment, he squints, struggling to see. Then, his expression shifts to a faint and knowing smirk on his face.

"Look at you," James says, smirking.

Darius stares.

"Didn't think I'd ever see you again," James continues.

Darius says nothing.

"Gotta admit... figured you'd be dead by now."

While listening to him, Darius steps closer.

James chuckles, a dry, wheezing sound, and said, "Guess I was wrong."

After a pause, Darius reaches into his pocket and pulls out a vinyl record.

James frowns and asks, "What's that?"

Darius walks to the dusty record player. Slowly places the vinyl. It clicks, and a scratchy hum fills the room.

Then, *"I Always Love My Momma"* begins to play.

James laughs in a raspy and bitter voice. "You're serious?" he says with a laugh.

Darius stares at him with a blank expression.

James shakes his head. "Boy, you're still living in the past."

Darius tilts his head slightly. "The past never left me," he says softly.

James chuckles again. "She's dead, kid," he says.

Darius freezes for a moment. "And you can't change that," James adds coldly.

Darius grips the edge of the record player. His knuckles turn white.

James leans back, still smirking. "You gonna kill an old man in his bed?" he asks.

Darius says nothing.

"Go ahead. Do it," James says with a laugh.

Then, after a long silence, Darius pulls out a knife.

James doesn't flinch. "That's all you got?" he asks.

Darius steps closer.

James locks eyes with him. "Your mother begged, you know," he says, grinning.

Darius stiffens.

"Cried like a damn child," James added.

Darius' fingers tighten around the blade.

"Always thought she was too soft," James adds.

There is a brief pause, and then James grins wider.

"Guess you are too," Darius lunges.

The knife slashed, cutting deep and fast. James gasps, clutching his stomach. Darius pulls the knife back.

James laughs, even as blood spills over his hands. "That's all you got?" he repeats.

Darius grabs him by the throat. James's laughter chokes off.

Darius leans in. "I want you to feel it," he says, steady.

James' eyes widen.

Darius presses the knife to his throat. "Like she did," he adds.

Then, after a minute, Darius slowly, painfully, presses the blade in. James gurgles, his body convulsing. Blood spills down his chest.

The song keeps playing. *"I Always Love My Momma…"*

Darius stares into James' eyes. He watches the light fade. Then, after a long silence, Darius lets go. James slumps, lifeless. The song reaches its final note. Darius steps back, his hands dripping red. He stares at the body and deeply exhales.

Then, he gives a smile, a small smile. Darius turns and walks out. Behind him, the record spins to silent.

Outside, the city streets are dark at night. The city feels divided. Protests are happening outside the police department.

Cardboard signs wave through the air:

"LET HIM FINISH THE JOB!"

"SOUL SLASHER = JUSTICE"

"END THE CLOWN KILLER!"

The crowd chants, some in support, others in fear. News cameras flash, capturing every second. Reporters stand in front of the chaos, speaking into their microphones.

"With yet another murder linked to the so-called 'Soul Slasher,' tensions continue to rise. While some call him a vigilante hero, others say he's nothing but a serial killer," a reported on TV says.

The screen flickers to footage of Darius' latest crime scene. A chalk outline. A record player is spinning in the background. Blood dripping down a wall in the shape of a clown's smile.

Inside an abandoned building, at night, Darius stands in front of a cracked mirror. His hands were steady, and his eyes were hollow. On the table before him, there is a jar of white face paint, a can of red spray paint, and a knife.

"No more hiding," Darius says.

He dips his fingers into the white paint, smearing it across his skin.

"No more masks," Darius adds.

He paints his entire face, methodically, like an artist finishing his masterpiece. His features twist into something… inhuman. He grabs the red spray paint and starts to paint... Schhhhht. A blood-red smile stretches across his lips. He tilts his head. He sees that in the mirror, the man he was is gone. Only the clown remains.

"You wanted a monster?" Darius smirks. He steps back, admiring himself. "Now, you've got one," he adds.

At night, inside the police station, there is a cramped, dimly lit room. Cigarette smoke swirls in the air. Detective Marsh leans over a cluttered desk, flipping through crime scene photos. Each one more brutal than the last. A clown's smile painted in blood. A record player spinning eerie 70s music. A trail of bodies—all of them were abusers.

His partner, Detective Rivera, tosses a file onto the desk. "We got a lead," Detective Rivera says.

Marsh glances up.

"A guy says he saw him," Detective Rivera adds.

"Where?" Detective Marsh asks.

Rivera pulls out a napkin. Scrawled across it: "Cloud 9 – old 70S club, midnight."

Marsh stares for a moment. Then, he grabs his coat.

"Let's end this," Detective Marsh says.

Later at night, inside Cloud 9 Nightclub—a dingy, 70s-themed club with flickering neon lights. A disco ball spins slowly overhead, and vinyl records hang from the walls. A soft funk song hums through the old, crackling speakers. The few remaining patrons are drunk and barely conscious.

In the center of it all stands Darius. He leans against the bar, slowly sipping a glass of whiskey. His painted face glows faintly under the dim red light, giving him a haunting look.

A shadow appears at the door. Detective Marsh steps inside, scanning the room. His eyes lock onto Darius. For a moment, everything stops.

Darius smirks. "Took you long enough," he says.

Marsh grits his teeth and reaches for his gun—but BANG! A bullet tears through the jukebox. Darius fired first. The music cuts off instantly. A silence follows, heavier than death.

"You didn't think I'd make this easy, did you?" Darius says.

Marsh steps forward. "You're done, Darius," Detective Marsh says.

"Am I?" Darius asks as he grins wide. "Because from where I'm standing... I've never felt more alive," he says.

Marsh narrows his eyes.

After a pause, Darius flips the table. Glass shatters, and Marsh dives behind the bar as bullets fly. Darius charges forward, and they clash. A brutal fight starts— knuckles cracking, furniture breaking, blood splattering. Darius grabs a broken bottle, swings it at

Marsh. Marsh dodges and punches Darius in the ribs. Darius laughs.

Darius stared him down. "That's all you got?" he says.

Marsh grabbed him by the collar and slammed him against the bar. Darius spat blood, smirking. "You fight like my old man," he says.

Marsh snarled and punched him again. Darius didn't flinch. "And you know what happened to him?" he asks.

Marsh reached for his gun, but Darius kicked it away. The gun skidded across the floor. Marsh lunged, but Darius was faster.

He grabbed a knife, slashed across Marsh's arm. Blood spilled. Marsh stumbled back. Darius grinned, licking the blood off the blade.

"Game over, detective," Darius says.

After a moment, Marsh spat blood, smirking. "Not yet," he says.

He kicked a stool into Darius' legs. Darius stumbled. Marsh grabbed a bottle—smashed it over Darius' head. Glass rained down. Darius fell to his knees, dazed.

Marsh pulled out his handcuffs. "You're under arrest," he says.

Darius breathed heavily. His face is still painted. His grin is still wide. Then, he laughed. A dark, guttural laugh. Marsh froze.

Darius stared up at him. "You think this ends with me?" he asks.

Marsh frowned.

"You really think people will forget?" Darius tilted his head, eyes burning with pride. "I'm not a man anymore." He leaned in closer. "I'm a legend."

A long silence. Then, sirens wailed outside. The cops were here. Marsh kept his gun trained on him. Darius slowly raised his hands, a twisted smile painted across his face.

After a heavy silence, Darius knelt on the floor, his painted face cracked with blood. A gun is aimed at his head. Detective Marsh stood over him, breathing hard. His arm dripped blood from the knife wound.

Outside, sirens screamed. The flashing red and blue lights leaked through the broken windows, painting the walls like some twisted carnival.

Darius tilted his head, smiling. "You should've killed me when you had the chance," he says.

Marsh gripped the gun tighter, his hands shaking. "Shut up."

Darius let out a dark chuckle. "What's wrong? Scared?"

"I'm not scared of you," Detective Marsh adds.

Darius smirked. "Then, pull the trigger!"

A long beat, the gun quivered in Marsh's grip.

Darius laughed. "See? You can't."

Marsh clenched his jaw, finger twitching on the trigger.

"Because deep down, you know I'm right," Darius says.

"You're a goddamn psychopath," Detective Marsh says.

"And yet half this city is cheering for me," Darius adds.

Marsh snarled. "That ends tonight."

A sudden sound—THUMP. THUMP. Boots are getting closer. A distant voice on a megaphone.

"THIS IS THE POLICE! COME OUT WITH YOUR HANDS UP!" Swat Commander says.

Darius tilted his head back, listening. A slow grin. "Well, well. The cavalry's here."

Marsh's eyes flickered toward the door. Outside, shadows moved. Silhouettes of SWAT officers stacking up. Rifles raised.

"Stay down," Marsh whispered.

Darius laughed again. "Oh, Marsh…"

His fingers twitched. A glimmer of steel, a knife hidden under his sleeve. "You really think I'm gonna let it end like this?" Darius says.

Slash! Darius lunged forward. Marsh twisted to avoid him, but not fast enough. The blade sank into his side, and he let out a grunt of pain. Darius grabbed him, spinning him around—Bang! Marsh's gun fired. A mirror shattered behind them. For a moment, everything paused. Marsh staggered back, clutching his ribs. Darius, breathing heavily, tightened his grip on the knife—then charged again.

Outside, red dots appeared on the club's entrance. The SWAT team, decked in black armor, waited for the signal.

"Go, go, go!" Swat Commander says.

Inside the club, a loud BOOM echoed as the door exploded inward. Smoke filled the room, and flashlights cut through the darkness. Automatic gunfire ripped through the air. Darius dove behind the bar, bullets whizzing past his head. SWAT officers moved in, advancing tactically.

"DOWN ON THE GROUND! NOW!" Swat Officer says.

Darius grinned, his body trembling with excitement. "You want me down?"

A single bullet tore through his shoulder. He stumbled back, laughing. Another shot at his thigh. His body jerked, but he didn't fall.

Marsh watched in disbelief. Darius kept standing. "Not yet," he said, laughing through the pain.

A volley of bullets ripped through the air. Darius was hit in the chest, stomach, shoulder, and leg. Blood soaked through his clothes. But he refused to go down. His legs wobbled as he gripped the bar, struggling to stay upright. "Not. Yet," he growled, his teeth clenched. His breath came in ragged gasps. His knees buckled, and finally, he dropped to the floor. A pool of blood spread beneath him.

His body twitched, each movement a struggle. The SWAT officers closed in, their steps heavy and relentless. Marsh staggered forward, clutching his wound, barely staying on his feet. Darius tilted his head up, his vision blurred, his ears ringing. The room spun around him. Somewhere, in the distance… A song played. Soft. Faint. *"I Always Love My Momma."* A tear slipped down his cheek. Then, he saw her.

Darius saw a soft light in his dreamy vision. His mother stood before him, smiling. Her warm eyes were filled with love.

"My sweet boy," his mother says.

His lips trembled. "Mama…?"

She knelt beside him, cupping his face. "Shh… It's okay, baby," she says.

Tears fell from his eyes. "I tried… I tried to fix everything."

She nodded, wiping his tears. "I know," Darius' mother says. She placed her hand over his heart. "But it's time to come home now."

His body trembled. His chest rose and fell. The music swelled. Her voice became a whisper.

"Let go, baby," Darius' mother says.

He stared at her, his body weak. His smile faded. Then, a final breath. A last heartbeat. Darius' head dropped, and his body went still. The music stopped. A long, deafening silence followed.

Detective Marsh watches as the light in Darius' eyes flickers out. A hush falls over the room. The SWAT officers lower their weapons. The legend is dead. A single tear rolls down Marsh's face, not for the man, but for the boy who never had a chance.

Chapter 9

A montage of news starts playing on the TV. The world reacts.

"The infamous 'Soul Slasher' has been confirmed dead after a violent standoff with police," a reporter on the TV says.

Images flash across the screen: candlelight vigils held in quiet remembrance, murals of Darius painted on city walls, protests demanding justice. News anchors debate whether he was a hero or a monster.

"While many mourn the loss of their so-called vigilante, others celebrate the end of a terrifying chapter in the city's history," the reporter says.

The camera cuts to Detective Marsh, walking out of the police station, his arm in a sling. A reporter shouts a question.

"Detective Marsh! Any final words on Darius Carter?" a reporter asks.

Marsh pauses, the silence stretching long between them. Then, barely above a whisper, he speaks. "He never really had a choice," Detective Marsh says.

He turns away, and the screen fades to static.

Inside the Cloud 9 nightclub, the room is still. Darius' lifeless body lies sprawled on the floor, his chest no longer rising. His painted face, cracked and smeared with blood, is frozen in a grotesque grin. The permanent, haunting expression of a man who embraced his darkness or was consumed by it. Red and blue lights from the police vehicles outside flicker over his face, casting shadows that make his painted features seem almost... alive. A slow, eerie drip of blood falls from his fingertips, landing on the wooden floor. Each drop echoes in the silence.

Moments later, Detective Marsh stands a few feet away. His breath is ragged, and his side wound throbs, blood seeping through his fingers as he clutches it. His vision blurs, but he refuses to look away. His eyes are locked on Darius—a man so feared, so hated. And yet, lying there now… he just looks like a kid. Marsh sways slightly, his balance unsteady. His partner, Detective Rivera, rushes over, gun still drawn.

"Jesus Christ… Is he dead?" Detective Rivera asks.

Marsh doesn't answer. He just stares. Rivera follows his gaze and sees the twisted smile frozen on Darius' lips. A shudder runs through him.

"Sick son of a bitch is still grinning," Detective Rivera says.

Marsh lowers his head, his thoughts burst like a storm. *Who was he, really? A monster? Or just another broken man, lost in a city that never gave him a chance?* His hand trembles, and blood drips from his fingers. Outside, the press swarm like vultures, cameras flashing in the night.

Chapter 10

Outside the city streets at night, news reporters fill the screen. A young reporter, Lana Stokes, stands outside the crime scene, microphone in hand.

"Breaking news, Darius Carter, the man infamously known as the *Soul Slasher*, is dead," Lana Stokes says on the TV.

Soon after, crowds gathered outside police barricades. Some holding candles, others holding protest signs.

"For weeks, the city has been divided—was he a hero, or a nightmare?" Lana Stokes says.

The camera pans over murals of Darius spray-painted on city walls. One mural depicts him as a savior—a vigilante who fought for the abused. Another portrays him as a demon, blood dripping from his grin. Opposing voices rise, arguing in the streets, each side fighting to define him.

"He stood up for people who couldn't fight for themselves!" protester 1 says.

"Are you insane?! He was a murderer!" protester number two adds.

A fight breaks out, chaos erupts, and now the city is divided.

Inside Detective Marsh's apartment, it's dark and silent. The only light comes from the glow of the TV screen. Marsh sits on his worn-out couch, bandages wrapped around his side. A half-empty whiskey bottle sits on the table, and his gun rests nearby. On the screen, the same news broadcast plays. Images of Darius, his frozen smile, stare back at him.

"What will Darius Carter be remembered as? A legend? Or a nightmare?" Lana Stokes says.

Marsh takes a slow sip of whiskey. He doesn't know the answer, and that terrifies him. The camera slowly zooms in on Marsh's face, capturing the weight of everything pressing down on him.

Later that night, inside a small apartment, a flickering TV casts unsteady light across the room. The same news report plays. The room is dimly lit. On the couch, a young woman, early 20s, sits curled up, watching the screen. Her eyes are red and swollen. A fresh bruise marks her cheek. She clutches a pillow tightly to her chest. The footage on the TV cuts back to Darius' face. That final grin, frozen and eternal. Her breathing slows.

Something shifts in her eyes. She leans forward. Her hand trembles, but she doesn't reach for the remote. Instead, she reaches for the kitchen knife on the table. Her fingers wrap around the handle tightly. The blade gleams under the glow of the lights.

"The world never changes. Only the monsters do."